HIM

ANVI.L

Here we go again,

with your mixed signals

and my overthinking.

Contents

Prologue

· 'Now Ill ask you' He said

"she just hummed"

· 'suppose I propose you what will be your answer'

"I dont know may be yes may be no

· 'Nope you have to answer clearly'

"Then its a no"

· 'okkk; he replird

'what will be your answer if i propose you' she asked him

· Ill say yes to you he said

somewhere at the bottom of her heart that answer made her happy
He likes you priya her friend said
"He doesnt like me iam a just a timepass for him "she said with a laugh from her lips and sadness in her eyes.......
"

1

a girl was waiting at bus sop suddenly a boy came and wishpered will you come with me the girl turned and seeing the person she sighned in relief "God ajay you scared me ".

haha sorry priya said Ajay 'stop laughing and come we have to reach your home fast or else uncle gonna scold you again ' said Priya .

they stared walking suddenly the boy asked suppose if i propose you what will be your answer and instantly her pervet heart said yes yes yes but she shutted her heart and said its a no ajay and what will be your answer if i propose you now she asked him its a yes from my side he said her heart did a happy dance.

Priya woke up from her sleep and smiled remembering her dream its not a dream its her beautiful past but her smile vanished as she remembered yesterday's news that " Indian captian Ajay shah and super model vanya arora announced their relationship through instagram "

she know it will happen someday she know she isnt that important in his life and she kmow he didnt love her but her stupid heart doent ready to accept that.cleaning her face.

She sat on her study table and " enough Priya you have to moveon from him "she thought to herself , she know its not easy but she have to do it for her family and for herself.

She started cleaning her cupboard and removing his memories from her life but she cant its too difficult for her while removing.......

2

while removing she found her old dairy in which she wrote about him she opened and started remembering her old days with him

When Priya said to her friend about Ajay and his question about proposal her friend Liya instantly said He likes you Priya she said giggling but priya didnt agree with her because she know about him and

then she said he doesnt like me Liya iam just a timepass for him she said ina joking manner with a smile on her lips sadness in her eyes but Liya is Liya she kept on blabbering that he cares for me and blah blah ....

she came to present by shaking her head she wanted to forget him but will she stop loving him no she cannot its been 10years since she fall in with him .They both were good friends when her friend asked her what is he to you Priya reffered him as a closefriend.

She used to share every damn thing to him even he is used to share with her but not as much as her ;he even got angry when she stopped sharing her thoughts with him.She thought that was his care but now she came to kmow that it is not.

He is not good in studies.His dream was to become Cricketer .Every day she si used to pray for him and his dream.He took time to tell his father about his goal and as he know he wont agree.

Somehow he covinced his father . And he agreed tooo.

All of his friends and my friends were happy because we know he will achieve his dream no matter what and he achieved too. But he became that popular that he even forget about her .

3

"I always remember you as the most beautiful mistake of my life"

"she decided to move on from him but she cannot unlove him "

she opened her diary and started writing,

DEARSOMEONE,

I DIDNT KNOW WHAT IAM FOR YOU ;

BUT FOR ME YOU ARE SOMEONE WHOM I'LL THINK ABOUT EVERYDAY

YOU ARE SOMEONE FOR WHOM I'LL PRAY FOR SAFETY AND TO REACH YOUR GOAL;

YOU ARE SOMEONE WITH WHOM;

I WANT TO SHARE EVERY DAMN THING I DID

YOU ARE SOMEONE WITH WHOM ;

I WANT TO SPEND MY EVERYDAY

YOU ARE SOMEONE FOR WHOM ;

I'LL STAY EVEN AFTER YEARS WHEN YOU NEED ME

yours love

Priya.

Priya...... called her mom . coming mom.....

sighning she closed her diary and kept it in store room along with his memories .

"THE END"

4

"THANKYOU TO ALL READERS"

5

I HOPE YOU LIKE MY SHORT STORY

6

THIS IS MY FIRST STORY I TRIED MY LEVEL BEST

THANKYOU AGAIN IF YOU LIKE THIS BOOK PLEASE LET ME KNOW AS I WILL CONTINUE THIS BOOK WITH PART 2

www.ingramcontent.com/pod-product-compliance
Lightning Source LLC
Chambersburg PA
CBHW061412160726
47995CB00002B/579